1

Puzzle Cube

Romilly,

Best wishes

Sarah Clark

Sarah Clark

Clink
Street

London | New York

Published by Clink Street Publishing 2019

Copyright © 2019

First edition.

The author asserts the moral right under the Copyright, Designs and Patents Act 1988 to be identified as the author of this work.

ISBNs:
978-1-913136-80-2 paperback
978-1-913136-81-9 ebook

For Oliver

1
The Riddle

Welcome to the Puzzle Cube.
The place to settle scores.
Carvings have been stolen,
from each of my four drawers.
The pieces match a building,
that's my only clue.
Return them to the drawer,
I'll have another rhyme for you.

'It's a riddle!' Sophie exclaimed, as she finished reading the text that was etched onto the lid of the mysterious wooden box.

'Open the top drawer,' Tom urged, shivering with excitement. 'See if there's anything inside.'

Gently, Sophie eased the drawer from the box and examined the contents. Along a trough at the edge of the drawer were several wooden pieces, carved into the shape of noughts and crosses. She picked up a cross and ran her fingers around its smooth edges. The exterior of the box looked old and battered but the carvings were pristine, as though they have never been used.

'Wow!' Sophie whispered under her breath. 'This is amazing. How long has this box been hidden in our shed?'

Tom wasn't listening. He was busy placing the pieces into the centre of the drawer, where nine grooves had been sculpted to fit each piece.

'Three carvings are missing,' Tom remarked, looking at the empty grooves in the drawer. 'Two noughts and one cross.'

'But where do we start looking?' Sophie wondered.

Before Tom had the chance to reply, a white light appeared around the edges of the shed door. Its piercing beam shone through the dark night and made the door edges glow. Tom took two steps backwards and tried to hide behind his sister.

'What is that?' he cried, pulling Sophie away from the glare.

'It must be Mum or Dad,' Sophie said and braced herself for another telling off. Now I'm in for it, she thought. How do I explain being in the shed at midnight?

But the door didn't open and no one called out. The light grew stronger until the inside of the shed was as bright as day.

'It's not Mum or Dad,' Tom whimpered, his stomach flip-flopping with fear. 'And it's getting closer. What is it?'

Sophie tried to peek through the small, dirty window but the light was so dazzling, she couldn't see the garden, or their cottage. Who could be out there at this time of night?

'There's only one way to find out who it is,' she declared, tightening the knot around her long ponytail, and walking bravely towards the door.

She was abruptly stopped by Tom, who grabbed her shirt and dragged her backwards.

'What are you doing?' she hissed. 'You nearly choked me!'

'You can't open the door,' Tom spluttered. 'We don't know what's out there.'

'We can't stay in the shed all night, either.' Sophie said, shielding her eyes from the blinding glare. 'We have to see where the light is coming from.'

'No, we don't,' Tom said, stubbornly.

Sophie bit her lip. She knew she shouldn't have told Tom about the box.

'You didn't have to come down to the shed tonight,' she snapped, losing patience with her younger brother. 'I said you'd be too scared. I found this wooden box and I can solve the puzzle by myself, so don't try and stop me. For all we know, the light could be a clue. I'm going to investigate.'

'I'm not going out there,' Tom declared.

'Then you'll be left alone in the shed,' said Sophie, knowing the effect her words would have.

Tom shook his head and clenched his fists in frustration. Ever since Sophie turned thirteen, she thought she knew everything. And once again, she was about to bully him into something he didn't want to do. His hands shook as he gripped the belt hook on his sister's jeans and he blindly followed her through the shed door, towards the light.

2

Through the Portal

When the door opened, the light was so bright that Sophie couldn't see anything. She had to trust that the garden would be where it had always been and she stepped out, expecting her feet to sink into the grass. With her arms stretched in front of her, she stumbled forwards towards the light. Then, to her amazement, she walked through it. Gradually, the light became fainter and her surroundings swirled into view.

'What on earth?' she muttered, blinking furiously.

As soon as Tom's eyes adjusted to the daylight, he spun around frantically. Desperately searching for something he recognised.

'What have you done?' he yelled at Sophie. 'Where are we?'

Sophie had no idea. She gazed around in bewilderment. The garden and the shed were nowhere to be seen. They had been replaced by a bustling, noisy city. She and Tom found themselves at the top of a wide set of stone steps, overlooking a busy street.

Behind them was a grand old building, with enormous columns at its entrance. Sophie was completely baffled. Where was their cottage?

There were people everywhere, scurrying around the street below. It all looked vaguely familiar and yet very strange.

'Sophie! Take me home, now!' Tom exploded.

Sophie tried to ignore him. She was too engrossed in the scene before her. Why does it look so weird? she thought. Something is out of place.

'Answer me!' Tom yelled, shattering her daydream. 'What just happened? Where are we?'

'Look at the people,' Sophie murmured, her mind spinning with unanswered questions.

'Look at the people?' Tom repeated, incredulously. 'I'm not interested in the people! Look at the buildings. Look at the cars. None of it belongs in our garden!'

'Exactly!' said Sophie, her eyes fixed on the view. 'Look at the buildings and the cars. They look a hundred years old.'

'What do you mean?' Tom began and then stopped. He watched a young girl selling flowers from a basket over her arm and realised how scruffy her old-fashioned clothes were. The women buying the flowers was wearing gloves and a hat, even though it was a warm summers day. In fact, everyone seemed to be wearing a hat.

'Why are they dressed like that?' he asked.

Sophie couldn't answer him. She loved an adventure but even she felt out of her depth. Where were they? And even more bizarrely, *when* were they? Nothing that Sophie could see made her feel as though she was in the present day. Everything looked dated and from another era.

'I think we're in a different place AND time,' she said hesitatingly, knowing how stupid that made her sound.

Tom refused to listen. 'Stop talking rubbish and tell me how we're going to get home. You got us into this.'

'You didn't have to come!' she yelled. 'I don't know where we are but look around you, everyone is dressed as though it was a hundred years ago.'

Tom couldn't deny that Sophie was speaking the truth. The old-fashioned cars, the strange clothes, the double-decker buses with stairs on the outside. It all looked so peculiar.

'Maybe we're on a film set?' he said.

'Now who's talking rubbish?'

'What do you suggest then?'

'I suggest you shut up for five seconds while I think,' Sophie shouted, regretting that she had ever let Tom come with her. His timid behaviour drove her mad. It was hard to believe he was only two years younger than her.

'You need to think fast and tell me how we're going to get home.'

Grabbing Tom by the shoulders, Sophie positioned her face a few inches from the end of his nose.

'I don't know how we're going to get home,' she said, pausing between each word for emphasis. 'But I suggest we find out where we are and search for the pieces from the Puzzle Cube.'

Tom looked at her as though she were mad.

'The Puzzle Cube?' he almost choked on the words. 'I couldn't care less about the Puzzle Cube. I want to go home.'

'But finding the missing pieces could be the way to get home,' Sophie yelled, completely exasperated.

Tom's wide eyes stared at her. 'How are we going to do that? We don't even know where we are.'

'Then we need to explore and figure out where we are,' she said, grasping for a plan. 'That may give us a clue of where to start looking for the carvings.

'You're insane,' Tom replied. 'There's no chance of finding three tiny carvings in the middle of this city!'

'Do you have a better idea?'

Tom stepped away from her and tried to calm down. He didn't have a better idea but he wasn't going to admit it. Sophie is always doing crazy things, he thought, but she's gone too far this time.

'Let's go down to the square and have a look around,' she suggested, sensing Tom's indecision.

They descended the stone steps, feeling very conspicuous in their modern clothes. As they reached the bottom, Tom turned to look at the building behind them and immediately recognised it.

'It's St Paul's Cathedral!'

'Then we're in London,' said Sophie in disbelief. 'This is amazing.'

Tom shook his head.

'It's not amazing. It's crazy. And just because we know where we are, it doesn't help us get home.' He didn't want this discovery to distract Sophie from finding a way back to their shed.

'We need to find out what year it is,' said Sophie, almost tripping over her words with excitement. 'Look, there's a boy selling newspapers. There'll be a date on the paper.'

'Wait, Sophie,' Tom interrupted. 'We don't want to draw attention to ourselves.'

But Sophie didn't wait. She darted across the square to where the newspaper stall stood. Tom followed, muttering under his breath. He could see there was a young boy in front of the stall, with a huge sheaf of papers over one arm. The other arm was held aloft, waving a newspaper, as he announced the headline of the day.

'Daughter born to Duchess of York!' proclaimed the boy. 'A baby Princess!'

Sophie arrived at the stall and attempted to read the date on the paper that was balancing over the boy's arm but the print was too small.

'Could I see the date on your newspaper?' Sophie politely asked and without waiting for a response she pulled the paper towards her face.

'Oi!' yelled the boy. 'You need to pay for that!'

'Oh, I don't want to buy it,' Sophie explained, 'I just want to find out what today's…'

'Thief!' cried the boy at the top of his voice. 'Thief!'

Sophie dropped the newspaper in horror. She stepped back and held out her empty hands. The crowd around the stall fell silent and everyone stared.

'No, no!' she stuttered. 'I'm not trying to steal it.'

'Then hand over your money,' demanded the boy.

'But I don't have any money,' Sophie said quietly.

'See?' The boy addressed the growing crowd. 'She was trying to steal my newspapers. Call the police!'

From the faces in the crowd, Sophie could tell that they believed the newspaper boy. She could also see Tom shaking his head as he backed away towards the cathedral. Sophie copied him and tried to reassure the boy that she had no intention of taking a paper without paying for it.

'Grab her!' cried the boy, as he watched Sophie inch backwards. 'Grab her, before she gets away.'

'Run!' yelled Tom, turning towards St Paul's and praying his sister would follow him. 'Run, Sophie!'

3

On the Run

Sophie had every intention of running but as she began to move, a hand gripped her shoulder and another grabbed her ponytail. She tried to turn and see who had hold of her but the grip was too tight.

'That's her,' cried the newspaper boy. 'Don't let her go.'

Sophie glanced around the growing crowd of people and knew she wouldn't be able to barge through them. Then she had an idea. She stopped struggling and stood very still. She felt the hand relax on her shoulder, then she dived to the floor. The grasp on her shoulder released but the hold on her ponytail was strong. Reaching up to her hair, she gave a strong tug and yanked herself free, losing a chunk of hair in the process. Once on the ground, she crawled along the pavement, ducking through and around the legs of people in the crowd.

A stout, angry man pushed people aside as he pursued Sophie. As he got closer, he threw himself onto the ground and attempted to grab her legs. Sophie kicked and wriggled as his hands caught her jeans and trainers. By now, she had reached the edge of the crowd and with a fierce bunny kick, she rose to her feet and began running. Never in her life had she run so fast. Behind her, she could hear the man scrambling to his feet. In front of her was St Paul's and Tom waiting by the steps.

'Run,' she yelled at the top of her voice. 'I'll catch up.'

Tom was more than happy to keep running and Sophie was soon by his side. Together, they tore along the pavement at the side of the cathedral, past the gardens and down the busy street. There were so many people on the pavement and they all seemed to be walking the opposite way. Clumsily, the children darted and weaved their way along the crowded footpath.

'Are we still being followed?' Tom yelled.

Sophie looked behind but it was too difficult to see through the crowd. She thought she could see someone trailing them but didn't want to alarm Tom.

'Don't know,' she replied. 'Just run!'

They sprinted along the main road until they came to a small, side street. Tom turned into it and Sophie followed. Towards the end of the street was a narrow passageway, which Tom almost ran past, until Sophie caught hold of his jumper and pulled him into it.

The passageway was filthy. Rotting rubbish formed mountains on either side of its narrow walls and the stench made Sophie gag. She pulled the neck of her t-shirt over her nose to try and hide from the smell, as Tom leant on his knees, gasping for clean air. Breathlessly, they watched people passing by on the street and prayed that they hadn't been followed. But after five minutes, there was no sign of the man who chased them and Sophie began to relax.

'That was worse than the 100-metre sprint on sports day,' she said, trying to make light of their situation.

Tom glared at her furiously.

'It's not funny, Sophie. What if you'd got caught back there?'

'But I didn't.'

'What if you had?'

'No point, worrying about what might have been,' she said infuriatingly. 'How was I to know he was going to accuse me of stealing his paper.'

'We're lucky to escape in one piece,' said Tom in disgust, 'and now we're completely lost.'

'How can we be lost, when we have no idea where we're meant to be heading?'

Tom stared blankly at his sister. This was turning into a living nightmare.

'At least I know what year it is,' Sophie said. 'I saw the date. It's 1930.'

'How does that help us?' Tom asked.

'It's more information than we arrived with and it means that a lot of the city will be recognisable to us.'

'And how well do you know your way around London?' Tom sneered.

'I know that St Paul's is near the River Thames and that's where we should go.'

'Why?'

'Because from the river we can get our bearings and plan what do to about these puzzle pieces.'

'How is that going to help?' Tom asked, crossly. 'We're meant to be hunting for some noughts and crosses. The riddle said they were in a building. We're not going to find them in the river.'

'OK, let's start searching in St Paul's,' Sophie said slyly, knowing what Tom's reaction would be.

'I'm not going back there again!' he exploded.

'Then what do you want to do?'

Tom couldn't think of anything and he was tired of being led on a wild goose chase. But he eager to leave the smelly alleyway. Reluctantly, he followed Sophie and retraced their steps until they neared the cathedral. Then Sophie dragged him across the busy road and he trotted behind as she marched with purpose down another jam-packed street.

As they walked along, Tom stared around with anxious curiosity. The buildings were covered in adverts for products he'd never heard of. Everything was strange and different. From the way people dressed, to the peculiar vehicles they drove. And there was Sophie, still striding ahead, oblivious to her surroundings. It seemed to Tom that she was enjoying herself.

'Come on,' she called over her shoulder. 'We need to get to the river before it gets dark.'

Tom trudged after her, feeling very despondent. Trying to find the river was a ridiculous plan. Miserably, he traipsed behind, dodging people on the pavement as he tried to keep up with Sophie. As he walked, he became more tired and hungry with every step. Then a horrible thought occurred to him. They had no money to buy food. They had no place to sleep. He cursed Sophie. This was the most stupid thing she had ever done.

'Sophie, wait,' Tom called and ran to catch up with her. 'Even if we find these pieces, then what do we do?'

Sophie flapped away the question with her hand.

'One problem at a time.' she said airily.

'We've got more than one problem.' Tom said angrily. 'We have nothing to eat, nowhere to sleep, no money and no way of getting home.'

'I don't have all the answers'

'All the answers?' said Tom in amazement. 'You don't have any answers!'

Sophie bit her lip and tried to stop herself from screaming at him. Why had she agreed to show him the Puzzle Cube? This adventure may have been frightening on her own but at least she wouldn't have to put up with his constant whinging. She was sick of having to be in charge of her brother all the time.

'Do you even know where you're going?' Tom asked.

Sophie stopped walking and smiled.

'Yes, I do,' she said. 'Look.'

As promised, she had led them to the River Thames.

4

The Hooded Man

Sophie was very proud of herself for finding the River Thames. She ran over to the railings to take a good look at London from the river. Darkness was starting to fall but on each side of the water, lights were appearing as the buildings came to life. She could still see the boats chugging up and down the busy water way and in the distance, were the bridges that spanned the river.

'Aren't you going to say anything?' Sophie asked. 'Like, "Well done"?'

'Well done,' Tom declared in a flat voice. 'Now what do we do?'

'You could be a bit happier about it.'

'Why?' asked Tom. 'We're no closer to finding our way home. We're just lost by a river now.'

Sophie had heard enough.

'You're so negative,' she exploded. 'At least we know where we are, what the year is and we can plan what we are going to do next.'

'What we need to do next, is find somewhere to sleep,' Tom shouted. 'Have you thought about that?'

Sophie took a deep breath. Normally, she would have retaliated with angry words but even she acknowledged they had to find shelter for the night. After her encounter with the newspaper seller, she was reluctant to approach anyone for help.

She pulled Tom closer to the railings and forced him to survey their surroundings. 'I know we have to find somewhere to sleep and put a plan together,' she began.

'And find some food,' interrupted Tom.

'And find some food. But look around you. We're in London! Doesn't the city look amazing at night, with all the twinkling lights?'

'No,' answered Tom, as he briefly glanced at the view. 'It doesn't.'

'I know it's a bit scary right now but we'll find some food from somewhere and then we'll form a plan and…'

But Tom wasn't listening. He stood utterly still, staring directly across the water. His brown eyes bulged, as his mouth gaped open.

'What's wrong?' Sophie cried in alarm, taking hold of his shoulders and trying to turn him towards her. 'What's the matter? Are you OK? Tom? Answer me!'

Tom couldn't speak. He couldn't move. All he could do was stare at the building on the other side of the water.

A cold shiver went through Sophie as she became very aware of how alone they were in this city.

'Tom, you're frightening me. What's wrong?'

Robotically, Tom lifted his arm and pointed a finger. Sophie's eyes followed but she couldn't understand what had caused such a reaction. On the other side of the river stood a long, squat brick building with a narrow tower protruding from the centre of the roof. Her eyes ran anxiously over the bricks and the windows but she couldn't grasp what was causing Tom's panic.

Then, suddenly, she realised what Tom was staring at and her hand shot over her mouth in surprise.

To her amazement, she saw the windows at the top of the tower were designed in the shape of O, X and O. Now that it was dark, the light from inside the building streamed through the glass and perfectly illuminated the shape of the noughts and cross.

'That's incredible!' Sophie exclaimed. 'It matches the pieces. They must be inside.'

'We'll have to wait until morning to look for them.' Tom said. 'We can't go creeping around there at night.'

They both stared at the glowing windows. Tom leant on the railings feeling weak with relief. Sophie shared his feelings and was just beginning to relax when she became aware of someone watching them. She tried to peer at the shape from the corner of her eye. A tall figure, shrouded in a huge hooded cloak was edging closer to where they stood. When Tom noticed this, he immediately stopped talking and stepped behind Sophie.

The figure leaned towards them, its back was bowed and a hand stretched out from beneath a grey, tattered sleeve. It seemed to beckon them over. Sophie began to move but Tom held her back.

'What are you doing?' he whispered. 'It could be a crazy person.'

'What do you think is in their hand?' Sophie murmured. 'I can't see.'

'Neither can I but I don't think we should find out.'

'We have to,' said Sophie and stepped forward.

The face was completely hidden by a hood which flopped over the head and towards the chin. From beneath the fabric there was a coughing sound.

'Well done,' croaked an old man's voice. He stretched his arm closer to the children and unclenched his fist.

Tom's heart almost burst with joy. Despite being terrified of this apparition, he wanted to hug it. There, resting on the palm of the hooded man's hand, were three wooden pieces. Two noughts and one cross.

5

Home Again

Sophie could hardly believe her eyes. They had found the pieces! The missing pieces! Maybe they would be able to return home after all.

Forgetting his fear, Tom approached the man and took the carvings.

'Thank you!' he cried. 'Thank you, so much!'

Sophie snatched one of the crosses and examined it.

'It's exactly the same as those in the Puzzle Cube,' she exclaimed.

'But now we've found them,' said Tom 'how do we get home?'

Sophie shrugged her shoulders and returned the wooden cross to Tom.

'For goodness sake, don't lose them.'

As she spoke, Sophie realised she was standing in pool of light. She turned to see where the light was coming from but it became so bright she had to close her eyes against it. When she opened them again, she was back in the shed, at the bottom of their garden.

Blinking quickly, she tried to readjust her eyes to the darkness.

'Tom!' she shouted, afraid her brother had been left behind in London.

'I'm here,' he replied and gave Sophie an uncharacteristic hug. 'I'm so happy to be home.'

'I wonder what time it is?' Sophie said. It was still pitch-black outside. 'Can you find the torch?'

The two of them felt around the floor of the shed until Tom picked up the torch and shone it on his watch.

'It's 12:15am. The same time it was when we left.'

'I can hardly believe what's happened.' said Sophie. 'Were we dreaming?'

'Not if noughts and crosses are real in dreams,' replied Tom and he shone the torch onto the three tiny pieces of wood in his hand.

'What an incredible thing to happen,' Sophie whispered.

'No one would ever believe us,' Tom said.

'You must never tell anyone,' cried Sophie in alarm. 'It's our secret!'

'I wasn't going to tell anyone. I'm just saying that even if we did, no one would believe we'd been to London tonight. They would think we were mad.'

'That's fine by me,' said Sophie, a loud yawn escaping her lips, 'because I don't want anyone to know about it.'

Tom yawned too and then realised how tired he was.

His watch may say it was only 12:15am but he felt as though he had been awake for days.

'I'm going to bed,' he declared, hoping Sophie did too. He didn't want to walk through the garden on his own in the dark. He'd had enough adventures for one night. All he wanted to do was climb into bed, pull the duvet over his head and sleep for a million years.

'Before we go, we should put the pieces back where they belong in the Puzzle Cube.' Sophie said.

Tom felt so sleepy, he would happily have left the pieces until the morning but he could see that Sophie wasn't going to leave until the pieces were safe. He directed the torch towards the box on the workbench. The lid was still open as they had left it. He handed the pieces to Sophie and she placed each one in its correct space. The first puzzle was complete.

'Now can we go to bed?' Tom asked.

Sophie didn't answer. She was examining the underneath of the box lid.

'The riddle has gone!' she exclaimed. Tom saw that she was right, the lid was smooth and there was no sign of words ever having been carved into it.

'Let's look again in the morning,' he suggested. 'It will be much easier in daylight.'

Grudgingly, Sophie closed the lid. Then she pushed the drawer, containing the noughts and crosses, back into the box. The drawer locked shut with a tiny 'click'.

'We should put it back under the work bench,' Sophie said but Tom resisted.

'No one is going to find it before we come back tomorrow,' he argued. 'Let's just go.'

'No. Help me put it under the bench.'

Together they struggled to manoeuvre the heavy box under the workbench. Tom could hardly believe that a box this small could weigh so much. When it was safely tucked out of sight, they walked back to the house.

'I wonder how we get the second drawer open,' Sophie mused.

Tom didn't care. He was only too glad another drawer hadn't opened this evening. He wanted to get back into the house before his parents realised he wasn't in his bed.

6

Mr Ravenwood

When Tom opened his eyes the following morning, the sun was streaming around the curtains at his bedroom window. For a moment, he was confused about where he was and then, with some relief, he realised he was in his own room. The events of the previous evening felt like a dream. All the images and sounds of London still swirled around his head. Did they really travel back in time? Lying in bed on this sunny Saturday morning, Tom struggled to believe it.

Outside his room, on the landing, he could hear his mother trying to wake Sophie.

'Come on, sleepyhead,' his mother called. 'It's 11 o'clock. Half the day is almost gone.'

If Sophie replied, Tom didn't hear her response. Then his door opened and his mother entered the room.

'Time to get up,' she said, as she opened his curtains, 'I don't know why you two are so tired this morning but if you don't get up soon the day will be over. Come down to the garden when you're dressed. You can help me with some weeding.'

'OK,' Tom replied and his mother left to knock on Sophie's door again.

'Are you awake yet, Sophie?' Tom heard his mother shouting. 'I need some help with the gardening, so get moving.'

Sophie had been trying to ignore her mother's voice and had almost succeeded in going back to sleep, when she heard her mother mention the gardening. Groaning, she turned over and pulled the duvet above her head. Then a second later, she flung the duvet on to the floor and jumped out of bed in dismay. If her parents were tidying the garden, they would have gone into the shed for the tools. And if they went into the shed, they might discover the Puzzle Cube! Reaching for last nights' clothes, she dressed as she ran into Tom's room.

'Tom, get up!' she yelled but Tom was already out of bed and half dressed.

'What's the matter with you?' he asked sleepily.

'Mum and Dad are working in the garden!'

'So?'

'They'll be using the tools in the shed!'

'The Puzzle Cube!' cried Tom in alarm. Grabbing his jumper, he ran towards the stairs.

Sophie was already ahead of him, jumping down the stairs two at a time. What a disaster it would be if their father found the Puzzle Cube before they had discovered what was contained in the other drawers.

When she arrived in the garden, Sophie could see her father trimming the edge of the lawn and knew he'd already been into the shed. Trying very hard not to sprint down the garden, she made her way to the shed and glanced inside. To her relief the Puzzle Cube was still safely hidden under the old cabinet.

Her mother was pulling up shallots from the vegetable patch and as soon as she saw Sophie, she asked her to pick some of the broad beans.

'I'd like you to take them over to Mr Ravenwood this afternoon,' her mother instructed.

Sophie pulled a face.

'Do I have to?' she asked. 'He gives me the creeps.'

Sophie's mother frowned.

'That's not very nice. Mr Ravenwood was very kind when we moved into this cottage. It's thanks to him that we met so many of the lovely people in the village.'

'Did Mr Ravenwood live here for a long time?' Tom asked his mother.

'His family lived here for years,' his mother explained. 'And I'm sure he still misses the garden.'

'I'll go with you, Sophie,' Tom volunteered. He was slightly intimidated by Mr Ravenwood but it was better than weeding the garden.

His mother had prepared a basket with a selection of their home-grown vegetables, which Sophie unenthusiastically carried to Mr Ravenwood's that afternoon. His house was on the other side of the village and as they drew near to the row of small terraced houses, they could see Mr Ravenwood standing outside his property.

'What's he doing?' asked Tom nervously, slowing his pace.

'It looks like he's knocking on his own front door,' Sophie laughed. 'I told you he was bonkers.'

'We could always tell Mum that he wasn't home,' Tom suggested.

Sophie shook her head. 'I'm not carrying this basket all the way back home again while it's full of vegetables, it's too heavy. Come on.'

'Good afternoon, Mr Ravenwood,' Sophie called as they reached his house.

The old man turned slowly and stared at them both, tugging on his long grey beard. He took so long to reply that Tom thought he hadn't recognised them. He was about to reintroduce himself when Mr Ravenwood finally spoke.

'What are you two doing on this side of the village?'

Sophie handed him the vegetable basket and told him their mother had sent them.

'Always very kind, your mother,' Mr Ravenwood muttered and took the basket, which caused him to stoop even further forwards. 'Give her my thanks.'

'I will,' said Sophie and turning to leave, she noticed

a pile of wood working tools at her feet. 'Is there something wrong with your front door?'

Mr Ravenwood tugged on his beard again, then rubbed his craggy face. He seemed to be struggling to find an answer.

'It's new,' he said slowly, 'and it don't fit proper. Needs planing.'

'Do you need any help?' asked Tom, who loved doing woodwork at school.

'No. I can do it meself. Just takes time, that's all.'

'OK.' said Sophie quickly, before Tom could utter another word. 'We'll be off then. Goodbye.'

Mr Ravenwood grunted and carried the basket into the house. As soon as they were out of earshot, Sophie turned on Tom.

'Why did you offer to help? We'd have been stuck there all afternoon!'

'He looks too old to be fixing that door by himself.'

Sophie rolled her eyes. All she cared about was getting back to the Puzzle Cube. The last thing she wanted was to waste time helping an old man fix his front door. Her parents must have finished working in the garden by now and she was desperate to open the second drawer.

'Come on,' she called to Tom, as she quickened her walk. 'I want to get home.'

'Do you think there will be another riddle for us to solve?'

'Yes, and we need to be more prepared this time. We should take some food with us and a map.'

'How can we take a map when we don't know where we're going?'

Sophie hadn't thought of that. She had assumed they would be going back to London again but Tom was right, who knew which place they would go to, or which time period.

'It was a good job I knew the way to the River Thames,' she said, trying to divert attention from her mistake. 'If we hadn't got to the river we'd probably still be stuck in London.'

Tom stopped walking. His feet felt as though they were glued to the footpath. That scenario had never occurred to him. What if they hadn't found the pieces? Would they ever have got home again? No one would have known where they were. They would have been stuck in the past for ever.

Sophie charged ahead, not waiting for Tom. She was on a mission to discover the next adventure.

7

The Second Drawer

Sophie was extremely disappointed to find her parents were still in the garden when she got home and worse, they were frequently in and out of the shed. Each time her father opened the shed door, the children held their breath and prayed the Puzzle Cube wouldn't be discovered.

After a busy day, where neither of them could escape the garden chores, they decided to meet up on the landing, after their parents had gone to bed. This time, Tom wasn't so afraid of walking through the garden in the dark. This time, he had much bigger concerns. What if they were transported back to the past but couldn't solve the riddle? What if they went back to when dinosaurs roamed the earth and were eaten! What if they got separated and he was left alone to find the pieces? The dark held no fear for him now. He was far more frightened of what would happen when the bright light shone again.

Later that evening, when the house was silent,

Sophie and Tom crept to the shed. As soon as they put the Puzzle Cube onto the workbench, the lid released from its lock. And there, carved on the underside, was a new riddle.

'What does it say?' Tom asked. As usual, Sophie had hogged the space in front of the box for the best view. 'Come on, read it out.'

Sophie cleared her throat and began to read.

> *So, you think you're clever,*
> *now you've solved my little test?*
> *Do you believe you're ready*
> *to attempt the second quest?*
> *British engineering,*
> *held aloft by bricks and mortar.*
> *Will lead you to a place,*
> *whereby the curve will meet the water.*

Neither of them spoke as they pondered the riddle. Tom was very excited that it had something to do with engineering. There were many historical feats of engineering that he would love to witness first hand.

Sophie, however, was feeling uncomfortable. As she read the first two lines, she felt as though the Cube was speaking directly to her. She did feel quite clever after their last adventure and she was very proud of how they solved the puzzle.

'It's almost like the Cube knows who we are,' she said.

'What do you mean?' Tom laughed. 'How could it know who we are? It's just a box made of wood!'

'It's much more than a box made of wood!' Sophie, exclaimed. 'And I think it's teasing us.'

'Don't be stupid! We have to solve the puzzle, that's all. And to do that, we need the second drawer to open.'

Click!

From an unseen lock, the second drawer sprang free. Gingerly, Tom eased it out of the cube and together they examined the contents. It looked very similar to the first drawer. There were grooves carved out for nine pieces but this time, all the pieces were the same.

'Three pieces are missing,' said Sophie, as she picked up one of the carvings. It looked like a letter 'n', with two solid legs and a flat top. She gave a piece to Tom. 'What do you suppose that's meant to be?'

The piece was very smooth, except for the four sharp corners of the flat top. The legs of each piece slotted snuggly into grooves that were hollowed out in the bottom of the drawer.

Tom was completely baffled.

'At least with the noughts and crosses, we knew what they were,' he said whilst studying the carving. 'These don't look like anything I've seen before. How will we know where to start looking?'

Sophie was just as perplexed but she didn't mention that to Tom.

'Once we know which place and time we're in,

we'll be able to make a plan,' she said, with far more confidence than she felt. 'Did you bring some snacks?'

'Yes.' Tom's pockets crunched as he patted them. 'I've got a small torch too.'

Quickly, Sophie re-read the riddle and tried hard to memorise as much as she could.

'What happens now?' Tom began but before he could finish, the gap around the shed door started to glow. This was the part he was dreading.

'Ready?' Sophie asked.

Tom didn't have an answer to that question, so he reached for Sophie's hand and together they walked cautiously towards the door.

8

The Mill

Before the dazzling white light had faded, Tom let go of Sophie and put his hands over his ears. The noise that assaulted his eardrums was deafening but he couldn't see where it was coming from. In fact, he could hardly see anything at all. He turned to Sophie and yelled at the top of his voice.

'Where are we?'

'In a cupboard!' Sophie shouted.

'What?'

Sophie prised Tom's hand away from his ear and yelled into it.

'We're in a cupboard!' Then she placed her eye against one of the many holes that were in the wooden cupboard door.

Even though the cracks in the door gave Sophie a good view of the space outside the cupboard, she wasn't sure what she was looking at. But she could see what was making all the noise. Before her stretched a long room, which contained machines as far as she could see. Although it was difficult to see very far because the air was full of tiny specs of white fluff.

It seemed to be some sort of factory. There were lots of men and women around the machines, who didn't seem to mind the noise. Then Sophie noticed the children. There were lots of them, some younger than she, crawling underneath the machines while they were still moving. None of the adults seemed to care that the children were in danger. At any moment, Sophie expected a child to become caught in the machinery.

Tom crouched down to look through a gap lower in the door. As he peered through the opening he saw white cotton thread stretched out in rows on the machines and large bobbins in baskets waiting to be threaded onto the loom. We're in a cotton mill, he thought excitedly. He could hear the shuttles flying across the looms, weaving the thread in and out of the weft. Each moving part clattered and banged so loudly, he thought the loom would break. He watched, fascinated, as each part moved in conjunction with the others, to produce a wide roll of cotton fabric. There were spinning wheels connected by belts and small cogs turning larger cogs. It was amazing.

Last year, his class had visited an old cotton mill. That mill had only one working loom but the man who operated it had worn ear defenders. None of the people Tom could see had anything to protect themselves from the noise, nor from the machines themselves. All the working parts were dangerously close to the men and women operating them.

For over an hour, Tom and Sophie watched the busy workforce. The workers never stopped and there was no opportunity to escape from the cupboard. Just when Sophie thought her head would explode from the relentless din, the looms began to slow down. The noise level dropped and a bell could be heard clanging above them.

'It must be the end of the shift,' Tom said. 'They're all packing up for the day.'

'Thank goodness for that, the noise is driving me crazy. We need to get out of here. I can't breathe with all that dust.'

'It's the fluff from the cotton,' Tom explained but Sophie wasn't listening. She was watching the workers leave the mill and planning an escape. As soon as the room was clear she opened the cupboard door and ran towards one of the many large windows. Tom followed slowly behind, his curiosity getting the better of him. He couldn't help but examine one of the looms. Wouldn't his teacher be amazed if he told her about this!

'Come on, Tom.'

Reluctantly, Tom walked towards Sophie but before he could reach her, a young boy appeared from beneath one of the machines.

Tom almost jumped out of his skin and his first reaction was to run to Sophie but then he saw the boy's face. He seemed just as terrified. Tom looked at the tattered rags the boy was wearing and realised how strange his own clothes must seem.

'Who are you?' the boy asked, his eyes darting over Tom. 'And what are you doing in here?'

'I'm Tom and that's my sister, Sophie,' Tom explained. 'We're trying to find the way out. Can you help?'

'It's no good going down them stairs,' the boy said, pointing to the staircase that the workers had used just a few minutes earlier. 'The foreman will be at the bottom of 'em and he won't take too kindly to you being in 'ere.'

'Billy!' a gruff voice shouted from the bottom of the stairwell. 'Get down here. Or do I have to come up to hurry you?'

'No, sir,' the boy replied quickly. 'I'll be down in a minute.'

'Who do you think you are, to keep me waiting!' the angry voice shouted and then footsteps could be heard climbing the stairs.

'It's the Foreman!' hissed Billy. 'You have to hide!'

Sophie raced towards the cupboard from which they had just escaped. But Tom span around looking for a place to hide, unable to decide which way to run. Now he wouldn't reach the cupboard in time.

From the safety of the cupboard, Sophie held her breath. She watched Tom's increasing panic as the footsteps became louder and he remained frozen to the spot.

'Get under the loom.' Billy instructed and, with seconds to spare, Tom squeezed under the silent machine.

The Foreman thundered into the room. 'Is your time more important than mine!' he bellowed at Billy.

'No, sir,' Billy replied calmly, although he was shaking inside. 'There's a problem with that loom. I wanted to fix it before I left.'

Sophie watched with admiration, as the young boy stood his ground before this terrifying man.

The Foreman stared at Billy and then at the loom where Tom was hiding.

'I won't be long,' Billy explained, trying to divert the Foreman's attention.

Without another word, the Foreman turned and left the room. Sophie opened the cupboard door and ran over to where Tom was hiding.

'Tom, it's OK to come out,' she reassured him.

Tom wriggled and crawled his way from under the loom. He thought of the children that he'd watched working underneath it while it was operating and shuddered.

'You should get out of 'ere,' Billy said urgently and herded them towards another staircase, that was situated behind the cupboard. 'Carry on till you reach the door at the bottom. I'll meet you outside.'

Down and round the staircase wound itself through the building, until eventually it stopped at a low door, that opened onto a dark lane. Gratefully, Sophie stepped outside and breathed in the fresh night air. Ten minutes later, Billy appeared.

'You two had a lucky escape,' he said, 'but you should be able to find your way home now.'

Tom and Sophie shared a worried look. It was pitch black. There were no streetlights. And they had no idea where they were.

Here we go again, Tom thought.

9

Billy

Billy observed the worried look that passed between Sophie and Tom. He could see they were scared but didn't understand why.

'You're not from round 'ere, then?' he asked.

'No,' said Sophie abruptly. She was always short-tempered when she was frightened. 'It's too difficult to explain but we're here on a short visit.'

'But we're not exactly sure where we are,' Tom added, as Sophie glared at him.

'You're at Wainwright's Mill,' Billy explained.

Tom and Sophie stared blankly at him.

'In Stockport,' he continued. When this didn't get a reaction, Billy started to laugh.

'Do you not know what town you're in?' he giggled in surprise.

'Which city is Stockport close to?' asked Sophie.

'Manchester, of course! Do you want to know which country you're in, too?' Billy chuckled.

Sophie scowled at him. She hated feeling stupid. But

Tom didn't care. He wanted to find out everything he could whilst Billy was willing to help.

'What year is?' Tom asked.

'It's 1841,' said Billy, shaking his head in disbelief. 'And Queen Victoria is on the throne.'

'Thank you,' said Tom, gratefully. 'That's a huge help.' Rummaging in his pocket, he pulled out one of the puzzle pieces and gave it to the boy. 'I don't suppose you've ever seen anything like this?'

Billy examined it, then shook his head. 'Can't say I have. Where did you find it?'

'It was given to us,' interrupted Sophie, before Tom could reveal any more information. She wanted to get moving towards the town and find somewhere to stay for the night. 'You've been very kind,' she said primly, 'but we really must be going.'

Tom stared at her. Where are we going to? he thought. It's so dark I can't even see to the end of the lane.

Thankfully, Billy came to the rescue. 'Where are you staying?' he asked.

'We don't know yet but we'll find somewhere,' said Sophie, just as Tom was saying.

'We don't have anywhere to stay.'

'Why don't you come home with me,' Billy suggested. 'We don't have much room but we'll find some space for you to sleep.'

'Thanks,' said Tom, hugely relieved that they wouldn't be sleeping in the bushes tonight.

But Sophie shook her head. She wasn't going to stay in a stranger's house. Her mother would be furious if she ever found out.

'We couldn't possibly impose,' she said, snootily. She wasn't completely sure what that meant but she remembered her mother saying it, when she wanted to turn down an invitation without hurting someone's feelings.

Tom knew Sophie would get annoyed if he disagreed with her but he was determined not to sleep on the street. If there was a chance of sleeping with a roof over his head, he was going to take it.

'Sophie, let's go to Billy's,' he begged. 'We can start the search in the morning. It's stupid to go wandering around in the dark. We don't know where we're going.'

Tom could see Sophie was wavering, so before she could object again, he asked Billy to show them the way.

Billy led them down the dark lane until they reached a row of narrow terraced houses. When they arrived at a house in the middle of the row, Billy pushed his shoulder against the front door and it wedged open just enough for them all to squeeze through. Then he threw his body against the door to close it.

As the door slammed shut, Sophie gazed slowly around the tiny room and shuddered with disgust. It was dark and dirty, with a few pieces of broken furniture and a small window that looked out onto the street. Two candles flickered dimly and cast eerie shadows across the walls. She thought of her lovely bedroom at home, with its thick, pink carpet and matching curtains. There was no floor covering in this room. Not even a rug. It smelt damp and there seemed to be children everywhere. Some were only a few years old and each one was staring at her.

'Is Dad home?' Billy asked one of the older children.

'He's already gone out,' came the reply.

Billy looked relieved.

'I saved you some bread and dripping,' the older child said, handing Billy a slice of grey bread coated with congealed fat.

Billy looked hungrily at the bread before offering it to Sophie and Tom. For once they were in agreement and politely refused. Billy devoured the food as though it was his first meal of the day.

Watching Billy eat the bread, Tom was reminded of the chocolate bar in his pocket. Slowly and carefully, he unwrapped it. Eight pairs of hungry eyes watched his fingers, as he peeled away silver paper. Snapping the bar into equal pieces, Tom handed one to each child and then to Billy. They all stared at the chocolate for a long time, as though they were unsure what to do with it.

'It's chocolate,' Sophie explained, putting her fingers to her mouth. 'You eat it.'

One of the older children licked his piece of chocolate and took a tiny nibble from one corner. The younger ones watched and when their brother's face broke into a huge grin, they followed his lead, taking small bites and savouring the taste.

As she watched the children enjoying the chocolate, Sophie's eyes pricked with tears. Then she immediately felt cross with herself for being so soft. She had never given much thought to people who were less fortunate than herself. Billy and his family were taking so much delight from a tiny square of chocolate, it made her feel guilty at all the pleasures she took for granted. She thought of the delicious biscuits and cakes her mother made every week and wondered if Billy had ever eaten a biscuit. Nothing in her life had prepared Sophie for this kind of existence. Before this evening, poverty had just been a word in her school books.

'What will you do tomorrow?' Billy asked, licking his lips for any remnant of chocolate.

'We'll go into the town and have a look around,' Tom replied. 'If you could point us in the right direction.'

'I can,' said Billy, with a wide grin. 'You've chosen a grand day to visit Stockport because the viaduct is opening tomorrow.'

'The what?' Tom asked.

'The viaduct. They've been building it for years. The first train will drive across it tomorrow and my Dad says that one day, people will travel by train from Stockport to London. Can you believe that?'

Neither Tom nor Sophie replied and Billy took their silence as confirmation of their amazement.

'It's the talk of the town,' Billy said proudly. 'Make sure you go to the viaduct while you're there. You'll be witnessing history. I wish I could go but the foreman would kill me if I wasn't at the mill tomorrow.'

'Yes, of course we will,' Sophie said politely, whilst thinking the last thing she wanted to do was watch a train cross a bridge. She wasn't sure where they would begin searching for the pieces but the town seemed like a good place to start. But before she could do that, she had to endure a night in Billy's home and she was dreading it.

10

The Viaduct

As the sun rose the following morning, Billy and two of his brothers prepared to go to the mill. Never in her life had Sophie been so glad to leave somewhere. She had hardly slept. All night, she had listened to the children coughing or crying and the church bell chiming every hour. They had slept on the floor of the front room and, all she thought of were insects and fleas crawling over her. What she wanted, even more than breakfast, was a warm shower and to feel clean again. Billy had made them feel very welcome but Sophie was itching to leave.

Tom had been blissfully unaware of Sophie's discomfort. He was thrilled to be in 1840s England. It had been incredibly exciting to stay with someone who worked at a real cotton mill. Billy had been very patient with all Tom's questions about the mill. Tom had listened, utterly fascinated, whilst Sophie shuddered at the distressing tales of Billy's working life.

When at last it was time to leave, Tom hugged Billy and thanked him. Sophie shook his hand and gave him the packet of crisps that had been tucked away in Tom's pocket. Even though she was really hungry. Billy explained how to get to the town and everyone said their goodbyes. Sophie walked quickly away, whilst Tom dawdled, turning around to watch Billy walk down the lane towards the mill. When he caught up with Sophie, they walked along the lane and down the gently sloping hill towards where the town lay, in the bottom of the valley.

'I'm so glad to be out of there,' Sophie said. 'This place is horrible. All I want to do is find those pieces and go home.'

Tom was astonished. He couldn't imagine a better adventure and longed to explore the town. As they strolled down the hill, he could see the tall chimneys of the mills and factories standing loftily against the horizon.

'I'd no idea there were so many mills,' he said. 'They're everywhere. It's incredible. We're in the middle of the Industrial Revolution.'

Sophie didn't comment. She saw nothing incredible about the view. All she saw was the dirt, grime and filth that came from the billowing clouds of black smoke. Every chimney was belching soot. She had no idea how Billy could work in one of those awful mills and then go home every night to that tiny house, with all his brothers and sisters crammed into one room.

They didn't have to walk very far towards the town before they saw the viaduct. It completely dominated the town and landscape. Its magnificent arches stretched across the valley, connecting the train line from one side of the town to the other and beyond.

As they got closer, they could see it was built entirely of bricks. Millions of them. Tom stared in awe at the enormous structure. Billy was right, he had never seen anything like it. There were twenty-two arches and nestled around them were more terraced houses and several mills.

Billy was lost in thought, admiring the workmanship, when Sophie suddenly lunged at him and pulled the puzzle piece from his pocket.

'What are you doing?' Tom yelled crossly.

'Look at the arches!' Sophie shrieked 'Each piece from the Puzzle Cube is the same shape. If we put all the pieces together it would form the viaduct.'

Tom stared at the odd shaped 'n'. Sophie was right! No wonder it had seemed such a strange shape. All the pieces had to be connected to make any sense.

'I bet the missing pieces are on the train that's going to cross the viaduct today,' Sophie said. 'Didn't the riddle say something about engineering held up by bricks and mortar? It must mean the train, up there.'

Tom looked doubtful. 'It did mention that but what about the water. You wouldn't find that on a train?'

'A steam train would have water onboard,' Sophie said with conviction, even though she had no idea if this were true. 'I say, we find that train.'

'I'm not climbing all the way to the top of the viaduct to search for those pieces,' Tom said, as forcibly as he dared. 'That's madness.'

'You stay here then,' retorted Sophie, and she walked towards the grassy hill that led to a makeshift station at one end of the viaduct.

11

Curves & Water

Tom watched, exasperated, as Sophie walked away from him. Why was she always so impulsive? And why did she never listen to his point of view!

There was a narrow, overgrown path that weaved up the side of the hill to the top of the viaduct but it was a very long, steep climb. Sophie was panting heavily by the time she reached the top, although she tried to hide this from Tom, who had eventually caught up with her and was hardly out of breath at all.

A crowd had gathered at the tiny temporary station, waiting to board the steam train. Ladies in long flowing dresses were accompanied by men in top hats and tail coats. They didn't seem like normal commuters.

'They look like they're going to a ball,' Sophie giggled.

Observing the men in their dark suits, Tom thought they looked as though they were going to a funeral. But there was an air of excitement and expectation. Everyone was talking animatedly to each other. No one seemed to notice Tom or Sophie as they zigzagged their way through the crowd, towards the train. As usual, Sophie was leading and they were just a few metres away from the tracks when Tom felt a hand on his shoulder.

'What do you think you're doing?' boomed a voice from under a tall black hat.

Sophie whirled around. Her heart almost stopped beating when she saw a man holding Tom by his shoulders. Quickly, she hid behind a group of chattering ladies and watched helplessly.

Tom froze. He couldn't think of anything to say.

'Er, um, I'm… er,' he spluttered.

The man tightened his grip on Tom's shoulders and dragged him to the edge of the gathering. When they were away from the ladies, the man pushed Tom roughly, sending him sprawling to the ground.

"I know what you are doing," he shouted, as Tom lifted himself from the floor. "You're trying to sabotage this historic journey. I know your type."

Tom shook his head violently but the man ignored him.

'Do you know how many of your sort tried to oppose this railway?' he asked, without waiting for an answer. 'Hundreds. But we defeated them all because the railways are the future.'

'I agree! The railway will improve everyone's lives.' Tom responded fervently, knowing that this wasn't strictly true but not wanting to debate the finer points of the argument with this madman.

'Then what are you doing here, dressed like a fool?' the man asked, suspiciously.

'I wanted to see the first train go across the viaduct,' Tom said, truthfully.

The man paused and considered Tom's answer but it didn't satisfy him.

'We don't want your sort here,' he said firmly, as he placed his hand tightly on Tom's arm and dragged him back to the top of the hill path.

'Don't let me catch you near here again!' he yelled and gave Tom a push which sent him tumbling down the hill.

Realising that Tom was free, Sophie dodged her way through the crowd and sprinted after him.

'Tom!' she called after him. 'Are you OK?'

Tom had already dusted himself off and was heading down the hill at high speed. He didn't slow down until the bottom of hill was in sight. Sophie could see he was very shaken but trying to put on a brave face.

'Can we go over the riddle properly now?' he asked crossly, as they reached the base of the viaduct.

Sophie blushed with guilt. 'Of course,' she replied.

'If the riddle means that the engineering is the train and the bricks and mortar are the viaduct, we need to search for the curve and the water.' Tom said.

'I agree,' Sophie replied.

Tom couldn't resist raising his eyebrows in surprise. 'Any ideas then?'

Sophie shook her head and they continued to walk the length of the viaduct in silence. As they strode ahead, the sky became darker and large spots of rain began to fall. Now they were at the centre of the viaduct, every arch they passed was so wide and tall, it offered very little protection from the rain.

'This isn't much fun,' Sophie declared, as the rain trickled down the back of her neck.

Tom agreed. Even his enthusiasm for this adventure was wearing thin.

'And now what do we do?' said Sophie furiously, as she pointed to the river that was flowing through one of the viaduct arches and preventing them from walking any further.

Tom groaned. How can this be so difficult, he thought, we've solved most of the clues. Where are the pieces?

'I'm fed up with this,' shouted Sophie. 'We've done everything!'

'Except to find where the curve meets the water!' Tom said, then began jumping up down and pointing his finger from the river to the top of the arch above them.

'Have you finally gone mad?' Sophie said, as she looked at him in disgust.

'This is it!' he cried. 'This is where the water meets the curve!'

Sophie gasped. Oh my goodness, she thought, is he

correct? She scanned her eyes over the curve of the arch and followed the bricks down to where they ended, by the banks of the river.

'You're right! You're right!' she exclaimed in delight and began to dance around.

Then, suddenly, there he was. The hooded man, shrouded in his long grey cloak, leaning against the wall of the arch.

'Oh!' Sophie said. 'You're here again.'

'Your brother was right,' the old man cackled and then began to cough. 'You could have saved yourself the climb up that hill.'

He held out his palm. Resting on it were the pieces that completed the puzzle. Sophie stepped forward to take them. The hooded man's head tilted slightly, not enough to see his face but to enable his words to be clearly heard.

'Next time,' he said slowly, 'read it carefully.'

'We will,' said Tom, who was feeling slightly braver around the old man now. 'Thanks for the advice.'

Just as he finished speaking, the familiar white light appeared. Tom and Sophie arrived, gratefully, in their shed. Both of them slightly stunned from their adventure. Especially Tom, who could still feel the grip on his shoulder from the madman at the station.

'It's good to be home again,' said Tom, as they walked up the garden path towards their cottage.

'It is,' Sophie replied, agreeing with him for once.

'We'll come back tomorrow and put the pieces in the cube. I'm too tired to even think about it now.'

But it was a week before they were able to complete the puzzle and during that time, Tom made an interesting discovery.

12

A Woodwork Lesson

All week, Tom and Sophie looked for opportunities to escape to the tool shed but their parents had other ideas. If it wasn't chores, it was homework. If it wasn't homework, it was housework. Somehow, there was always something that needed doing. They couldn't risk starting an adventure on a school night, so there was nothing for it but to wait until the weekend. Eventually, Friday finally arrived.

When Tom got home from school on Friday afternoon, his mother was waiting for him in the kitchen, with a freshly baked blackberry crumble.

'Can you take this to Mr Ravenwood and collect the basket you took last time?' she asked.

Tom pulled a face.

'Can Sophie come with me?'

'No, she has homework to do,' his mother replied.

'But I don't want to go on my own,' grumbled Tom.

His mother took no notice. Instead, she covered the top of the crumble and handed it to him.

'Make sure you're back in time for dinner.'

Tom intended to be home much earlier than that. He didn't want to spend a minute longer than he had to at Mr Ravenwood's. He and Sophie were planning to put the arch pieces back in the Puzzle Cube and read the new riddle.

Unenthusiastically, he took the pie and walked into the village. As he trudged along the country lanes, his mind was full of the last Puzzle Cube adventure. He had enjoyed his experience of the industrial revolution, especially exploring the cotton mill. The viaduct had also been amazing. He wondered whether it was still there and if his parents would take him to see it.

Before long, he had walked through the village and out to the row of terraced houses where Mr Ravenwood lived. As he got near to the house, he could see that Mr Ravenwood was working on his front door again. He coughed quietly as he approached, so he didn't startle the old man.

'You again,' said Mr Ravenwood, when he noticed Tom was behind him.

Tom handed him the blackberry crumble.

'Mum sent this and asked if I can take back the basket that we brought last time.'

Mr Ravenwood went inside the house without replying, leaving Tom standing by the doorstep. While he waited, Tom examined the new front door.

'Are making a new letter box?' he asked, when Mr Ravenwood appeared with the basket.

'New door didn't have one,' Mr Ravenwood muttered. 'I'm putting one in.'

Tom examined the tools Mr Ravenwood was using. They looked like something from another century.

'What's that?' Tom asked, pointing to a strange contraption that lay on the ground.

'It's a drill.'

'But where do the batteries go?' asked Tom.

Mr Ravenwood snorted. It was the first time Tom had heard him emit any sort of noise that was close to laughter.

'It's a proper drill. It don't need power.'

'But how does it work?'

Slowly Mr Ravenwood stooped down and picked up the drill. Tom thought it resembled the old whisk his mother occasionally used when she was baking. It had a handle on one side that turned a wheel but instead of a whisk at the end, it had a drill bit. Mr Ravenwood continued to use the drill on the door and Tom could see the corkscrew shaped shavings dropping to the floor, as the drill bit wound its way through the wood.

When he had finished with the drill, Mr Ravenwood asked Tom to pass him another tool. And before Tom knew what was happening, he was helping Mr Ravenwood to install his letter box.

They worked together without speaking, as Mr

Ravenwood grunted or pointed at the tools he required. After a while, Tom was allowed to use the drill by himself. At first, it felt clumsy and awkward but before long he was confidently drilling holes. For a while they laboured in harmony until the letter box was installed and Tom plucked up the courage to ask a question.

'What happened to your finger?' he inquired, pointing to the middle digit on Mr Ravenwood's right hand. The tip of which was missing.

'A saw took it,' Mr Ravenwood said, bluntly. Tom could tell he didn't wish to discuss it any further.

'Well, I'd better be going,' Tom said, suddenly feeling uncomfortable. 'Thank you for letting me help.'

Mr Ravenwood nodded and almost smiled.

'Thank your mother for the pie,' he called.

Tom raised his thumbs up in response.

All the way home, Tom's mind was on the Puzzle Cube. Now that the chores were done, it was time to open the next drawer.

13

A Wizard's Hat

Another painfully slow Friday evening dragged on. Tom and Sophie tried to occupy themselves, when all they wanted to do was run down to the shed and open the Puzzle Cube.

Eventually, their parents retired to bed and the house became silent. Sophie and Tom crept downstairs, their pockets stuffed with food, water and a torch. Tom still had the pieces from the previous puzzle and, when they got to the shed, he positioned them carefully in the second drawer of the cube. When they were securely in place, Sophie slid the drawer into the box and closed the lid.

'Do you think the riddle will appear soon?' Tom asked impatiently.

'Only one way to find out,' replied Sophie and she raised the lid.

To their delight a new riddle was carved onto the inside of the box. Sophie read it aloud.

Another riddle waits for you.
Sing praises, it's inspired.
A gathering of humble folk,
where hearts and minds are fired.
The stage is set, the story's told,
the crowd recite their lines.
Carvings can be found there,
if you open up your minds.

'It doesn't make any sense!' Tom exclaimed.

Sophie didn't respond. The contents of the third drawer were attracting her attention. The drawer released with its familiar 'Click' and slowly, she eased it from the cube. Tom immediately snatched a piece and examined it. The curious object resembled a twisted wizard's hat but instead of standing to a point, the top section was slightly bent to one side.

'They look interesting,' said Tom.

'And there are three missing as usual,' Sophie confirmed.

'Why isn't the light shining?' Tom asked, staring at the door.

'Who knows?' Sophie replied. 'But we should use this time to solve the riddle. I think it contains lots of clues this time.'

Tom nodded.

'"The stage is set, the story's told",' Tom read. 'It sounds like some sort of theatre to me.'

'But why would you find humble folk in a theatre?' questioned Sophie.

'I don't know but it also mentions the crowd reciting their lines. Maybe there's a pantomime and the audience are joining in.' As he voiced his idea, Tom felt convinced he was correct.

'Are hearts and minds fired in a theatre?' Sophie asked dubiously.

'They are, if it's a good show!'

They both fell silent. Sophie was mulling over the first verse of the riddle, whilst Tom was thinking it was typical of Sophie not to accept any of his ideas.

'A theatre doesn't make sense.' Sophie declared, after some thought. 'Why would you sing its praises?'

'Maybe you would if you'd really enjoyed the production.' Tom said, defensively.

Sophie shook her head. 'It just seems too easy.'

'You're just annoyed because you didn't think of it.'

'I am not!' Sophie retorted 'I don't agree with you, that's all. I think "singing praises" is a big clue. Where would you sing praises?'

'I don't know! If it's not a theatre, then you figure it out.'

'You're such a baby,' Sophie accused him. 'You can't listen to anyone else's point of view.'

Tom glared at her. That's rich coming from her, he thought, she never listens to anyone. He knew his theatre idea was the right one. The stage, the audience. It couldn't mean anything else. Reciting lines and singing praises. What else could it be, if not a play in a theatre?

Tom turned his back on Sophie and in his head, he tried to validate his answer. But the more he thought about it, something niggled inside his mind. Reciting lines and singing praises with humble folk. That wasn't a theatre. There was another place for that. Sophie was right. The 'crowd' wasn't an audience. It was a congregation.

'It could be a church,' he muttered. 'You sing praises in church.'

Sophie's gawped at Tom in astonishment.

'Yes!' she exclaimed 'And in church, you would recite your prayers with humble folk.'

Tom should have been pleased but he wished he'd thought of the church first and never mentioned the theatre.

'There could be hundreds of churches? Where would we start looking?' he asked.

Sophie was deep in thought. She felt sure they were on the right track with the church but were they missing something? Was there more to the riddle than they realised.

'Let's go over the riddle again,' she suggested.

Together they re-read it but neither could find any further clues. Tom examined the wizard hat carving and ran it through his fingers while he was thinking.

'The only line I don't really understand is the second one, "Sing praises, it's inspired,"' Sophie said.

'Praises are sung in church,' Tom replied. 'We've already solved that part.'

'But why would they be inspired?'

'Maybe the Cube thinks the riddle is inspired. It's certainly the best one we've had.'

As Tom spoke, the door glowed its familiar white light. Quickly, Sophie grabbed her notepad and copied the riddle. Tom put a wizard hat in his jacket pocket, squishing it in, along with the snacks he had brought.

'Let go,' Sophie said and made her way to the shed door.

As usual, once they walked through the door, the light steadily faded. Sophie blinked several times and waited for her eyes to adjust to the new surroundings. Gradually, it became clear that she was in a room in which the windows were boarded up. Whoever had nailed the boards across the windows hadn't done a very good job because sunlight shone through the many gaps. At first, Sophie thought she was in the front room of an empty house but as she peered through the gaps in the boards, she saw that the windows went from the floor to the ceiling.

'I think we're in an old shop,' she called to Tom.

There was no reply.

'Tom?'

Where was he? Sophie began searching around the room. Pushing over the old packing boxes that littered the floor.

'Don't mess around, Tom!' she cried angrily, her voice rising in panic. 'Where are you?'

But there was no answer. She was alone.

14

Separated

It took precisely two seconds for Tom to realise that Sophie wasn't with him. The room was unnervingly quiet, except for the short, sharp sound of his own breathing. Instantly, fear shot through his body and he sank, with a thud, onto an old wooden packing box. He was experiencing his worst nightmare.

'Keep calm,' he said aloud and took several, large gulps of air. But his hands still shook and his voice quivered. What was he going to do? In his head, he replayed the last few seconds in the shed, wondering what had gone wrong. Where was Sophie? Why wasn't she here?

Did he still have the puzzle piece? He jumped up and checked his pockets. Yes, the piece was safely in his pocket, along with the snacks. Then he remembered that Sophie had a copy of the riddle and he slumped back down on the box.

His thoughts reversed at highspeed to recall the conversation he and Sophie had had in the shed. What were they looking for? A church. How was he going to find that? He couldn't recollect a single word of the riddle and the only clue he had was the puzzle piece.

For the first time, he looked around at his surroundings and realised he was in a disused shop. There was an old, dusty counter and some shelving against the walls. The windows had heavy wooden boards across them but he could still see part of the street outside. On the other side of the street were shops, probably similar to the one he found himself in, except those shops were open for business. Moving to another gap in the window boards, he glimpsed the familiar road markings of dashed white lines that are found on any modern street.

'I've not gone back in time at all,' he muttered, experiencing the odd feeling of disappointment and relief. At least he wasn't going to stand out in a crowd. That thought was quite comforting.

Pacing around the small room, he tried to gather his thoughts. What would Sophie do? he wondered. As he walked, he ran the Puzzle Cube piece around his fingers. This is all I have to solve the riddle, he thought, so I have to use it. He knew the pieces always resembled the building they were searching for, so there was only one thing for it. He had to ask for help. The shop directly across the road was a newsagent. It seemed like a good place to start.

Next door, in the other disused shop, Sophie was

almost hysterical. How could she return home without Tom? What would her parents say? She suddenly felt very responsible for her younger brother. It was she who had found the Puzzle Cube. She who insisted they solve the riddles. She who had teased Tom for being scared and reluctant to take part.

Even if she solved this riddle and found the pieces, how could she take them? That would leave Tom without the means of getting home. The only thing she could do, was to find the Hooded Man and explain their predicament. Maybe he would have some answers.

Reaching for the riddle, she smoothed out the crumpled page and pondered the part that had perplexed her before she left the shed. Why would singing praises be inspired, she wondered, as she tried to picture the triangular pointed hats with their spiral twist and crooked tips. There must be some connection. And then an idea hit her so forcibly, she almost fell over. Holding her breath, she thought it over. Did it make sense? Could this lead her to the missing pieces? Yes, it might.

'Oh, that's clever,' she chuckled. 'Inspired, even.'

Outside the newsagents, Tom was trying to pluck up the courage to venture inside. Once he stepped into the shop, he found it was very busy with people waiting to buy lottery tickets. There was a long queue at the counter, so Tom joined the back of it and rehearsed what he was going to say. While he waited, he noticed a poster for the town fayre, which told him he was in Chesterfield. Not that Tom had any idea where Chesterfield was but it was comforting to know the name of the place he was in.

'What can I get you?' the shopkeeper asked, when Tom reached the front of the queue.

'I don't want to buy anything,' Tom said quickly, 'but I'm looking for a church that has something to do with this wooden piece. Can you help me?'

The newsagent picked up the small wizard's hat and held it up against the light. The people in the queue behind Tom also observed the piece and suddenly, the shop fell silent. Tom felt the hairs stand up on the back of his neck. Everyone was staring at him. For what felt like an age, the shopkeeper didn't respond. Then eventually, he leant forward across the counter, until his face was uncomfortably close to Tom's.

'Are you trying to be funny?' he said in a loud voice.

'No,' Tom replied, quietly. Clearly, he had offended the shopkeeper in some way.

The shopkeeper stood upright, his large belly resting against the counter and he shouted out to the other customers.

'Does anyone know where the boy can find a church that looks like this?' and he held the piece aloft.

To Tom's amazement, everyone started laughing. Then the shopkeeper saw the genuinely puzzled look on Tom's face and rolled his eyes.

'I'll give you some directions, shall I?' he said. 'Go out of my shop, turn left and look up.'

Some of the customers giggled at this. Tom muttered his thanks, took the puzzle piece and escaped from the shop as fast as he could.

As soon as he was on the street, he looked up towards the left and realised why the shopkeeper had thought he was so stupid. There was a twisted church spire, towering over the shops and streets beneath it. Tom shook her head and his cheeks burned with embarrassment. How had he missed it before he went into the shop? Tom put his hands over his face.

'That's probably the most embarrassing thing I've ever done,' he said to himself, not caring who heard, as his cheeks glowed a bright crimson. 'I'll never be able to come back here again.'

He walked quickly towards the end of the street and arrived at the churchyard. Before him, stood an old gothic church complete with a crooked spire, just like the Puzzle Cube piece. The building was magnificent but there was a more amazing sight that captured his attention.

'Sophie!' Tom yelled, running towards her and throwing his arms around her neck, almost knocking her to the ground. 'You're here! How did you find it?'

Relief flooded through Sophie as she clung onto Tom and it was a few moments before she could speak.

'How did you know to look here for the carvings?' Tom was delighted to see her but desperate to know.

Choking back her tears, Sophie found her voice. 'It's inspired,' she said with a smile.

'Inspired?' Tom was puzzled. 'Isn't that what the riddle said?'

'In. Spired.' Sophie repeated.

Tom pondered this for a moment.

'Oh, that's clever,' he cried.

'That's what I said,' Sophie laughed.

'I can't believe the spire hasn't fallen down,' Tom said, looking up at the church. 'It isn't just twisted, it's leaning to one side.'

'It's an incredible building,' Sophie said. 'Let's go inside.'

The main door was open but the church was spookily quiet.

'Do you think we should be in here?' whispered Tom, feeling that they were about to get in trouble again.

'Anyone is welcome in a church,' Sophie replied, but felt uncomfortable all the same.

They walked along the slate floor, into the church and down the nave, passing the many rows of pews. On either side of the church were huge stained-glass windows which were so beautiful, they took Sophie's breath away.

'This place is amazing,' Sophie said quietly.

'Why are we whispering, if we're allowed to be here?' whispered Tom.

Sophie shrugged her shoulders. It just didn't seem right to speak in a normal voice.

They had almost reached the altar when Tom spotted the hooded man. He was sat on a short set of spiral stairs that led to the pulpit. As the children approached, his right hand was outstretched with the three puzzle pieces in his palm.

'You solved this one quickly,' he grunted at them. His voice echoed around the church. Clearly, he didn't feel the need to whisper.

Sophie took the pieces and as she did so, Tom noticed something that made the air escape from his lungs in a whoosh. In the quiet church, it sounded like a gale blowing down the nave.

'What's wrong?' Sophie asked but Tom didn't reply. He couldn't take his eyes from the hand that proffered the wooden carvings. When he looked up, he could just make out the eyes of the man beneath the cloak. It was a startling discovery. He knew the identity of the Hooded Man.

15

The Story

The following day, Tom and Sophie met in the shed to discuss Tom's theory of the Hooded Man. They had returned the spire carvings to the Puzzle Cube and were keen to start the next adventure. But before they began, Tom wanted to understand what he had seen in the church. The next afternoon, after all the chores were finished, they locked themselves in the shed, away from their parents' radar-like ears. The conversation had begun quite calmly but it wasn't long before they were disagreeing.

'I just don't believe it,' protested Sophie. 'How could it possibly be him?'

'I know what I saw,' Tom argued. 'The tip of his middle finger is missing, just like Mr Ravenwood's.'

'That doesn't mean it's him. Lots of people have similar injuries.'

'It's him,' Tom stated fervently. 'I saw him looking at me when I noticed his finger. He knows we have figured it out.'

'How can it be him? How could Mr Ravenwood follow us through time?'

'I don't know but I swear on my life, the Hooded Man is Mr Ravenwood.'

Sophie was growing bored of arguing, she wasn't getting anywhere and it was clear that Tom wasn't going to change his mind.

'If you're so convinced it's him, you'd better go and ask him,' she taunted.

'All right, I will!' Tom shouted. Then immediately regretted being so impulsive. How was he going to ask Mr Ravenwood about the Puzzle Cube without appearing crazy? The experience with the shopkeeper in Chesterfield had been embarrassing enough.

A sly smile crept across Sophie's lips, she knew what Tom was thinking.

'I'll come with you,' she offered, sneakily.

Later that day, Tom approached his mother and asked if she had anything for Mr Ravenwood. She eyed Tom suspiciously.

'What are you up to?' she asked.

'What do you mean?' he replied, feigning innocence.

'You never want to go to Mr Ravenwood's.'

'Well, I er,' Tom fumbled for an answer. 'I er, helped him with his letter box last time and I want to see if it's finished.'

His mother looked disbelieving but fetched some scones she had made the day before and handed them to Tom.